WHISPERING TO HORSES

WHISPERING TO HORSES

An Amish Horses Novella

Thomas Nye

Horse Progress Days 2017

CROSSLINK
PUBLISHING

Whispering to Horses: An Amish Horses Novella

CrossLink Publishing
www.crosslinkpublishing.com

ISBN 978-1-63357-041-2

Library of Congress Control Number: 2015945869

This story is written as fiction. All names, places, and situations are a result of the author's imagination, or are used fictitiously. Any comparison to actual events, businesses, or persons living or deceased is purely coincidental.

Contents

THE FENCE

I n every Midwestern town, spring comes bustling with new life. Flowering trees drench whole communities with a perfume that stirs something within folks—something they knew as a child but soon forgot. Birdsongs are light and happy. Tulips emerge, touting bright colors. Lilac bushes hang with flowering clusters, dripping with a sweet aroma. Bees wake up buzzing, hurrying about and gathering pollen. Little toddlers make cheerful coos as they play with sticks and dirt, pick flowers, and drink in all of those ancient sights and sounds for the first time. Something very old becomes new in them. Deep within their tiny souls, they recognize a truth as old as time. Even a very small child knows it well.

There are a few locations in this world where antiquity and contemporary exist side by side; this is a story of one of those places. Years ago, when Matthew and Enos were young men, they labored together, putting in a fence between their farms. They dug holes, set posts, stretched wires tightly from post to post, all the while sweating under a hot summer sun. At the halfway mark, they had a long debate about whether or not to put in a gate.

Matthew declared, "A gate will weaken our fence."

Enos stated, "My grandpa taught me, 'Good fences make good neighbors, but a gate opens the way for help in time of need.'" That settled it. They placed a gate in the fence; however, it had never been used.

Enos was Amish, and his neighbor Matthew was not. In those days there was not much difference. Neither of the young neighbors had electricity; both farmed with horses. They even dressed something alike—suspenders, straw hat, and similar beards. The difference was in this: Matthew loved modern inventions and strove to be "up to date." Enos disliked change and made a clear effort to keep things "as they were." Matthew and Enos died in their nineties. This story is about their grandchildren and the fence with a gate that was never used.

For a very long time, the fence served the dignified purpose of keeping Enos's cattle from mingling with Matthew's. On one side of the woven wire, everything stayed the same. Over the fence, change was the only constant. Matthew was one of the first to purchase a newfangled engine on wheels; they called it a tractor. He could plow faster, plant more corn, and put up more hay, which led to buying more cattle and putting up larger, more modern barns. When the electrical company strung wires in their community, Matthew paid the price, tapping into it immediately. Enos and his church decided against it.

Matthew's children followed in his footsteps, always trying to keep up with every newfangled thing that came along—in fact, to the point where old Matthew himself began to miss the way things used to be. His daughter, Lucy, listened to phonographic records day and night. Her shadow could be seen through an upstairs window shade, dancing to those modern sounds. She discovered that she could make herself more beautiful with curlers and makeup. Her brother, Tommy, loved to listen to baseball on the radio. Static-laced voices shouted late into the night until Matthew purchased a black-and-white television. After that, Tommy watched games unfold right before his eyes. These games inspired Tommy to play ball himself. Not in the yard, as they used to do, but on a real team with uniforms, just like professional ballplayers. When Tommy was old enough to drive the family automobile, he and his buddies took laps around town in the evenings after ball games.

For entertainment, Enos and his large Amish family watched Matthew's modern world through the fence. Teams of Amish horses plowed on one side, but Matthew's tractor did "twice the work in half the time." Enos's boys took note that Matthew's new rig was so efficient. Tommy could plow a whole field in the morning and go to town, dressed in a uniform, to play ball all afternoon. Enos's daughters continued weeding the garden and hanging out their long dresses on a clothesline. They were jealous of Lucy's curly hair and brightly colored dresses. Nevertheless, they laughed the first time they saw her run out to a car in a pair of boys' pants. Enos's daughters used to enjoy looking at all of Lucy's brightly colored clothes flapping on her clothesline. About the time Lucy started wearing pants, clothes stopped appearing on the wash-line altogether. Enos's daughters worried that Lucy was sick, but word got around that Matthew had acquired a machine that dried clothes faster and better inside of the house.

Things grew very quiet on Matthew's side of the fence after Tommy and Lucy headed off to college. Enos's children were less distracted from their work, with only old Matthew to be seen over the fence. Matthew had newer, bigger tractors with air-conditioned cabs. He could farm the whole place by himself without even wearing a hat. One day, a crew with heavy equipment came in, and Enos's family speculated that Matthew was putting in a new set of hog buildings. They watched curiously as a whole row of houses were built in Matthew's hayfield.

Enos's boys guessed, "Tommy and Lucy must be moving back, and Matthew is building houses for their families?"

It turned out that strange people they had never heard of came from the city and took up residence in that row of houses. Enos went to a farm auction at Matthew's place and bought some of his old horse-drawn equipment.

Enos told his sons, "I talked to old Matthew at the auction. He said that Tommy and Lucy both live in big cities far away. Neighborhood gossip was that 'Old Matthew made so much money by selling off his land; he will never have to work again.'"

Things became really quiet after that. Those who lived in Matthew's suburban development left their houses early every morning, heading to jobs in town. Enos's family barely saw their new neighbors who didn't even get out of their cars to open a garage door. Their modern garage doors automatically opened and shut themselves.

One by one, Enos's sons found wives. Enos deeded part of his farm to one of his boys and built a farmstead for him a little further up that old fence row. Another son bought the acreage across the road. Soon, they all had large families of their own. The fence that Matthew and Enos built became the dividing line between suburbia and an Amish community. Little Amish children played on one side of that fence, and little English children on the other. Both sets of toddlers played with sticks and dirt while listening to bees buzzing from flower to flower, and birds twittering and fluttering in branches overhead. Sweet flowering trees and lilacs drenched their tiny nostrils with wonderful aromas. Children on both sides of the fence fellowshipped in those ancient truths. Around the age of ten, those things began to be scolded out of them. By the time they were sixteen, they had almost forgotten it. As adults, they denied it altogether. Except, during springtime, every year, there would be a fleeting, unguarded moment, and they would remember.

Chapter 2

A BIG PROBLEM

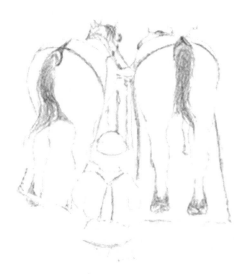

One particular springtime, shortly after old Matthew died, a young man moved into his old homeplace. His name was also Matthew, though he preferred to be known as Matt. This young man drove a nice car, and, like the others in his suburban development, he backed out of his automatic garage door early every morning. He raced to his occupation in the city until dusk, and then came bustling home in the evenings, with music blaring. On the first Saturday, Matt invited his buddy Ernie over for a meal. While hamburgers sizzled on the grill and music pounded out of his patio door, young Matt could be heard over the noise. "I'm gonna fix up this place and resell it."

"Why don't you want to live here? Isn't this where your mom grew up?"

"It doesn't mean anything to me! Besides, Ernie, I could sell it for a ton of money! That's if I can get you to do this landscaping job. I've got a crew coming to put siding on this week, all new carpeting and kitchen counters. This yard, though, it's pretty bad!"

Loud music kept up a good beat while Ernie thought about it. Finally, he called over the music, "I couldn't get to it for a month, and you're looking at $5000 at least for a project like this one. This is more of a field than a yard."

"Are you serious? Come on, Ernie, can't you help out a friend? I don't want to be stuck out here in Amish country. Don't you smell that?"

"What?"

"Look!" Matt pointed over the fence. A young Amish boy was driving a team of horses, pulling a little wagon that spit out a dark trail of manure as it went.

Ernie laughed. "Some people would love to sit and watch Amish working."

"Exactly, I'm gonna sell this place as soon as I can ... to someone who likes the Amish!" He looked at Ernie and asked again, "Can't you fit in this landscaping job somehow?"

"You need to learn some patience, Matt. If you can find someone who will do it cheaper and sooner, you better take them up on it."

Just about that time, the Amish boy rattled past, unloading manure. Matt called, "Hey, kid, don't get too close to the fence with that!" The boy waived.

Ernie said, "I don't know if he heard you, or if he thought you were being friendly."

"I don't know. He didn't look too smart."

A Solution

During the next week, young Matt tried contacting other landscaping companies, but they had longer waiting lists and higher prices. Every night, Matt walked on his newly inherited yard trying to think of a way he could do the job himself. He wore earbuds so he could listen to music instead of a creaking Amish windmill, or the bawling of their cattle. He happened to notice that same Amish boy plowing with a team of horses on the other side of the fence. A twinge of guilt pricked Matt's heart when he remembered yelling at the boy for hauling manure, but he quickly shrugged it off. A few days later, Matt was still brainstorming about how he could get his yard done. He sat alone in his empty house, which was filled with the noises of a crowd cheering in the ball game he was watching. During a commercial, he walked to the kitchen for another drink and noticed movement out of his window. This time the boy bounced on a small horse-drawn disc. The implement cut through dirt clods created by the plow and left a slightly smoother trail behind. An idea popped into young Matt's mind, but he quickly dismissed it as foolish. "Horse-drawn equipment can't make a yard smooth enough," he told himself, and believed it.

The very next afternoon, when young Matt came home from work, his car thumped with drumbeats as he pulled into his garage. Once more, he caught a glimpse of the Amish boy. He pushed the button that reopened his garage door and snuck around the corner for a better look. A team of horses plodded along, dragging something flat that the boy stood on. Surprisingly, the soil was becoming extremely smooth behind them. As the black team of horses came to a stop right next to the fence, a gentle breeze blew petals from a blossoming tree above Matt's head. Sunlight glimmered through those petals. A sweet aroma sparked something deep inside of him. He had been aware of his grandpa's Amish neighbors all of his life. He hadn't tried to talk to one of them since he was a boy, and he was almost thirty.

"Hey, young man!" Matt called.

"I'm not hauling manure," the boy sheepishly explained.

"Oh, I know, but can I talk to you for a second?"

"Sure, I'm resting my horses anyway." The Amish boy gave a slight smile, squinting up into the sun to see Matt's face.

"I would really like my yard to look like that field." He looked at the boy to see if he was tracking. "Would you be interested in doing some landscaping for me?"

"What do you mean?" The boy continued squinting.

"Maybe this wouldn't work, but do you think you could plow up my yard and finish it like you're doing this field?"

"I guess I could do that for you. I would have to finish planting this field first."

The Amish boy's eyes were so dark they were almost black. There was something of sorrow in them, and also of wisdom well beyond his years. Matt was taken aback by the look in his eyes. After an awkward moment of silence, Matt spoke again. "I wasn't asking you to do it for free; in fact, I will give you four big bills if you do a good job."

The Amish boy's dark eyes brightened for a moment. "My name is Eli."

"Hello, Eli, I'm Matt. Why don't you ask your parents about it and see what they say?"

"I'm sure it will be fine."

The boy seemed sad again as he said it, and Matt wondered if he was reading him right. Eli sat behind his huge black horses, staring at him, as though waiting for a better explanation. Matt looked at the Amish horses for a moment, stunned by how huge they were. He had been watching them out in an open field and hadn't thought about their size. Up close they towered impressively over the man and boy. The horses looked at Matt with almost the exact same expression the boy had.

Matt asked, "When do you think you could get it done?"

Eli looked away for a moment, as if calculating. "I will probably be done planting corn by this Saturday. If the weather holds out, we could start on your field next Monday."

Matt smiled. "That would be awesome! How long do you think it will take?"

Eli looked confused. "You are just going to plant grass seed in there, right?"

"Yes," Matt answered, almost as a question.

"Are you in a hurry?" the boy asked.

"Yes, I really want to get grass growing here as soon as possible, so I can sell this place."

"Okay, I will get to it as soon as I can." Eli stood up and walked around his horses and looked at the old fence. He walked a few paces along the wire and gazed at Matt's yard, and then he looked at the fence again. "There looks to be a gate here. If we could get that open, it would make everything better."

Matt walked along the fence on the opposite side. He hadn't noticed a gate there before. It appeared to be wedged in by dirt, which covered the bottom board. Grass was growing on the dirt.

"Do you have a shovel?" Eli asked Matt.

"I think so. Let me go see."

Matt jogged to his garage and looked around at his grandpa's old tools, found a shovel, and jogged back. Eli had already come up with a pair of pliers and cut through a wire that had been twisted tightly by Matt's grandpa years ago. Matt dug along his side of the gate, and then passed the shovel to Eli, who made quick work of it. Together, they lifted up the gate. Without even a word passing between them, Eli took one end and Matt took the other, and they dragged it along the fence. Matt pulled his end first and took it into his side of the fence. Eli stopped at the post and never stepped foot through the opening.

The young boy peered through the open gate and nodded. "Molly, Dolly, and I can do it."

"Are those your sisters?"

Eli laughed and pointed at his horses. Matt shrugged. "Oh yeah, I guess those are horse names." They both laughed. Eli went back to harrowing with his horses, and Matt went inside and turned on the TV, scrolling through the channels, searching for something good.

Chapter 3

HOPE

F or the next few days, Matt watched the weather like a farmer. He hoped that rains would hold off long enough for Eli to finish his planting. When he pulled into his drive, he didn't let the door shut behind him. Instead, he walked out to see how things were going for Eli. He spotted black horses, heads bobbing as they walked, coming up along the fence. Eli wasn't visible behind his huge team until he came up to where Matt was leaning on a fence post. Molly and Dolly stopped, almost as if they knew Matt planned to talk to the boy. Eli looked about nine by his size. His shiny dark eyes and sun-browned skin made him seem like a foreigner to Matt. His straw hat and suspenders added to the effect. Matt spoke first. "How is your planting going?"

"Good." Eli smiled.

"Do you think you will be finished by Saturday?"

"If it doesn't rain tonight," the little man answered wisely.

Matt added, "I hope it doesn't rain on Sunday either."

"That won't slow us down too much, unless it rains a lot." Eli looked at Matt for a moment, and then spoke again, "If I finish early Saturday, would it be okay if I bring Molly and Dolly over and pull a few of those weed trees that are growing in your yard?" He eyed Matt.

The older of the two looked along the fence row at small trees he hadn't noticed before. He then realized that there weren't any saplings on the Amish side of the fence. It instantly occurred to Matt that his neighbors might be annoyed about how things had been let go on his side of the fence. "Sure, you could pull those out if you want."

"It doesn't matter to me, but I thought that if you want your yard to look nice, we should get them out of there." Matt nodded in agreement. The boy whispered something, and his horses leaned into their harness, heading back to work.

Nuisances

Friday afternoon Matt was in a hurry to get home. He raced along, tapping one foot to music, pressing the gas pedal with his other. His phone vibrated and he pulled it from his pocket. Without shutting off his radio, he answered, "Hello. Oh hey, Ernie. What? You think you can fit me in at the end of the month?" While he talked, Matt came upon an Amish buggy at a place where he couldn't pass. "These blasted Amish! Why did I end up with a house in this area? Every time I'm in a hurry, I get behind a slow-moving buggy. I can't pass them because there is a double yellow line and we are heading uphill." Music thumped out of the radio, making it hard to hear what his friend Ernie was saying. Matt watched the horse crest a hill. As soon as the double yellow line disappeared, he pulled over to pass. With a screech, he swerved back, realizing a car was heading straight at him. "Just a minute, Ernie, I almost got killed right there. I can't get past this Amish woman." Finally, he had a brief moment where he was able to punch his gas pedal and roar past the annoying buggy.

Music continued to throb loudly as Matt yelled over it. "I think I found someone else to do my project." He slammed on his brakes, barely getting stopped at a four-way intersection. An Amish buggy had been there first and slowly clip-clopped into the lane ahead of him. "Oh, you have to be kidding me! I'm behind another Amish buggy!" A young Amish boy turned and looked at Matt's car as he tailgated him. "You'll be surprised at who I hired to do it." Matt paused for effect. "An Amish kid. Yeah, and he agreed to do it for a thousand dollars cheaper than you would." He pulled into his drive, searching the Amish field to see how Eli was coming with his planting. He climbed out of his car and walked toward the fence, still talking to his friend Ernie. "Yeah, I think he's gonna do a good job with it, too. You should see how nice his field looks." Matt leaned over the fence, holding his phone to one ear while searching for Eli. "Okay, Ernie, maybe it seems to you like I'm taking advantage of the kid, but he seemed excited about the project. What does it matter, anyway? As soon as I get this work finished, I can sell this house, make some money, and buy a nice condo where I don't have to worry about a yard." Matt leaned further over the fence, straining his eyes to see if he could see any horses, while Ernie talked. Matt snarled, "I know some people would love to live near these Amish, but not me." Matt turned and looked the other way; Eli was sitting right next to the fence, behind his horses. "Oh, Ernie, I gotta go. My friend Eli is here. Okay, bye."

"Hello, I didn't hear you pull up."

"Horses are pretty quiet." Eli smiled.

"It looks like you're about done, huh?"

Eli nodded. "If I didn't have to stop for chores, I could finish tonight." The boy seemed so young. Matt wondered what kind of chores a kid his age would have, especially after working in the field all day. He almost wanted to go say something to Eli's dad. "You're doing a nice job with this field, Eli." The boy smiled shyly and tilted his hat to cover his eyes. "I better not hold you up if you have chores to do." Eli smiled again and Matt stood to watch the youngster put his horses back to work. He thought he heard Eli whispering something. The glistening black horses rippled with muscle as they quietly stepped away. A faint clicking could be heard, and Matt assumed it was Eli's planter dropping kernels of seed corn.

The Gate

Matt woke up when sunlight hit his blinds. Though he normally slept in on Saturdays, he got up and slid open his living-room drapes, so he could watch the gate for Eli. He turned on some music to keep him company and got busy painting his kitchen ceiling. While keeping one eye on the window overlooking the gate, Matt finished rolling the center section and began to trim the edges carefully. His phone vibrated in his pants' pocket, and he dug it out. "Oh man, my mom again ... how am I ever supposed to get this work done?" He tapped the touch screen and said, "Hello, Mom." He held the phone away from his ear and looked at it, and then poked his finger into that ear. "Mom, you don't need to yell into the phone; I can hear you quite well." He set down his paintbrush and stood listening to her ramble for a while. "I know I'm not getting any younger, Mom. I don't need a wife right now; I'm doing fine on my own. No, I'm not worried that I'll never have any children. Kids these days are all brats anyway. All they do is beg for stuff and whine." He saw movement at the gate. "Oh, Mom, I gotta go. My man is here to work on the yard. Okay, I love you, too. Bye."

Eli's horses stood at the gate. Matt walked up. "Hello, Eli, are you ready to get started?" Eli nodded but his horses didn't move.

Finally, Matt motioned with his hand. "Come on through!"

He heard the Amish boy say something under his breath. Molly and Dolly arched their massive black necks and snorted. Both

16

horses' nostrils flared red and the whites of their eyes could be seen. Suddenly, they pushed through the open gate as though crossing a time warp.

"What just happened?" Matt asked the boy.

"I don't know," he said quietly. His horses pulled their little steel-wheeled cart up to where small trees voluntarily grew along the fence. Eli took a chain out from under his seat and hooked it about six or eight inches up the sapling's trunk.

"Are you sure you don't want the chain at the base of that tree?" Matt asked.

"Grandpa taught me to do it like this. It gives the horses a little cushion; as they pull, the tree trunk bends a little."

"Huh, I didn't think of that." After that, Matt stood back, as though watching an artist at work. He listened closely as little Eli almost whispered directions to his horses. They obediently waited while their driver hooked his chain. They strained impressively when asked, both massive mares leaning forward. At times all four front hooves came off the ground, and then plunging their weight forward, they dug deep until the tree surrendered its grip on the soil.

Eli quietly gave a command, "Ho." Molly and Dolly instantly stood still, looking like gentle ponies, dark eyes glistening. One larger weed tree grew entwined in the old fence. Eli looked at Matt. "We should use a saw on this one."

Matt nodded and headed to his garage to get some of Grandpa's old tools. Eli showed Matt the best way to lift the fence and cut below the wire. When Molly and Dolly had cleared every small tree, Matt pointed to one rather large tree on the edge of his property. "I guess I should get my chainsaw for that one."

"Don't cut down that apple tree." Eli's dark eyes seemed to be begging for mercy.

"I've tried those apples before; they're no good," Matt answered.

"They're applesauce apples." Eli smiled. "They ripen around the fourth of July. Leave that tree and let me come pick them. My mom will make the best applesauce you've ever eaten. She'll make some for you, too!"

"All righty, you talked me into it." Matt laughed and Eli smiled.

When Matt thought they were done for the day, Eli asked cautiously, "May I haul some manure over here?" Before Matt could answer, Eli quickly added, "We have some really old manure that's all decomposed and hardly smells at all."

"Are you wanting to get rid of it?"

"Oh no, it's the best stuff. Your soil isn't that good and this mulch will really make things grow. Since you are paying me $400, I want to make sure everything turns out right. If you want, you could go along and help me load it."

Matt looked around, as though someone would tell him whether or not he should. He worried that it may be awkward if he happened to run into Eli's dad. He decided that he didn't care what any Amish man thought, so he told Eli, "Okay." He followed the boy and horses on foot. They trotted across the newly planted cornfield.

Eli quickly hitched his team to an old steel-wheeled manure spreader. He carefully set a board across the wooden wagon box as a makeshift second seat for Matt. The non-Amish man couldn't help but smile as he took a ride behind Eli's shiny black horses. They trotted down a slope through a blossoming apple orchard. Something about the spring air, with sweet aromas, and sparkling rays of sunlight shooting through tree limbs drew a memory from deep within Matt. He looked around, wondering if he had been in this place before, or if Grandpa's farm used to be very similar. The heavy horses walked down between two old barns and came to a stop at a large pile. The younger of the two scrounged up a pair of pitchforks, and they set off loading the wooden box. Three little girls came down the hill in bright green Amish dresses and crisp white head coverings. They stood barefoot, watching Matt and Eli huffing and puffing to fill up their manure-spreader. Matt was happy when he was finally able to take his seat beside the boy and enjoy another horse-drawn ride up between barns and trees. He looked around at the neatly manicured garden and orchard. He saw a woman hanging wash on a clothesline. She peered around an Amish dress as they jostled past.

When they got back to Matt's place, Eli asked, "Do you want off?"

"I probably should for your horses' sake?"

"It won't make any difference for them if you do or don't." Eli looked at Matt. It seemed the boy knew Matt wanted to ride along. He pulled a lever on his side and asked Matt to pull a lever on the other. Eli whispered, "Get up." His horses leaned into their thick leather collars and a loud click-clack commenced. Matt watched the tines whirr and spin, flinging dried manure over his yard. The boy was right: if there was a smell, it was almost sweet.

Matt was almost disappointed when they took the last lap and finished unloading their cargo. They both disengaged their levers, and the older passenger climbed off. "Thanks, Eli; this was a good experience for me."

Eli smiled, his dark eyes shining. The boy pointed at the manure. "If you want, you could use a rake to even that out a little. I will plow it all under on Monday."

"Okay, I will. See you on Monday."

Eli nodded and breathed a quiet "Get up." Molly and Dolly stepped back through the gate and into their old-fashioned world again.

Chapter 4

MISUNDERSTANDINGS

After church, Matt and Ernie headed to their favorite restaurant for lunch. Music blared through his car radio as Matt bragged to his friend. "Ernie, this Amish kid thought I told him $400 for my landscaping job. He is working his tail off for peanuts!"

"Well, what's an Amish kid going to do with $400, not to mention $4000? What can I say, you lucky dog? If you're happy and he's happy with $400, leave well enough alone!"

In the evening, Matt got sick of watching TV, almost the way a child feels after eating candy all day. He decided to take a walk outside and look over his yard. Just as a red sun sat behind a set of Amish barns to his west, Matt heard something—a faint beautiful sound. He felt drawn to it. He walked toward those barns, silhouetted in the setting sun. When he came to the corner of his land, he could hear four-part harmonies floating out on a gentle breeze. It was a sound like he had never heard before. He had watched part of a show on TV about the Amish and learned that their teens gather on Sunday evenings to sing hymns. A lilac bush in his neighbor's yard sent a sweet smell his way. Matt felt like a child again for a moment. Then, he scoffed, "What a dumb way to expect teenagers to live." He headed back inside and scrolled through channels, searching for a good show.

Plowing

Matt pulled into his garage and ran inside to change. As soon as he got on his work clothes and shoes, he went to see how Eli was getting along plowing up his yard. Long slabs of black earth lay in thick rows. At the end of one row, Molly and Dolly were just turning around. Matt watched them lean into their collars and head toward him, with heads bobbing in a steady rhythm. Sweet onion smells rose up with an earthen scent. Matt watched a few nightcrawlers struggle to worm their way back into the black dirt. The ground looked quite rough, making Matt wonder if he had made a mistake. Eli came up smiling, as if trying to reassure the older guy that it was the right thing to hire an Amish boy, after all.

"Is it going to work okay?" Matt asked.

"Yes, fine. I can't get real close to the house, though."

Eli spoke quietly; Molly and Dolly leaned forward again, pressing into their leather collars. Matt watched, trying to see how the whole thing worked. His eyes traced out leather straps that made up horse harness. Driving lines made a large X between Molly and Dolly's bridles, which seemed odd. He examined the way Eli had hooked his horses to their plow. They had straps that ran along their sides, connected at their heels with a chain to a steel crossbar. That crossbar was in sections that were obviously made to allow for some give-and-take between horses. When Eli came back near Matt, there were some questions asked. "What is this part?" Matt pointed to the piece at the horses' heels.

"That is called an evener. It's designed to evenly distribute the weight of what the horses are pulling. Some horses are stronger and others walk faster, so one can be hooked closer than the other."

"Are you whispering to your horses?"

"My grandpa told me, 'Horses have very good hearing. If you speak very quietly, they will learn to listen carefully to what you are saying. If you yell a lot, they will learn to ignore you.' He used to tell me that I should make a game out of it and see how quietly I can whisper and still get my horses to respond."

"Interesting," Matt replied.

Eli quietly asked, "Are you planning to sell this place?"

"Yes, as soon as I can. It will help if this yard is in shape, with grass growing."

"Why do you want to move?" Eli asked, looking sad. Matt couldn't tell him that he didn't like living near the Amish, or that he was too lazy to keep up a big yard. He felt stumped and finally said, "I'm not sure."

Horsy Ride

Matt asked to leave work early on Tuesday and was thrilled when his boss gave him permission to go. He rushed home and found Eli discing up all of the thick dirt clods his plow had turned over. Both big horses had a small Amish girl riding on their broad backs, holding onto silver bars that stood up from thick black collars. The little girls were smiling and one of them chirped something in Dutch. Eli interpreted, "Marcille said, 'We are having a horsy ride.'" Matt gave the little girls thumbs up, and they looked at him as if they didn't know what that meant. He hurried inside and grabbed some popsicles out of his freezer and took four of them out. He gave one to each of the little girls and he and Eli stopped to eat theirs also. One of the little girls held a faceless doll that was dressed in Amish clothes much like her own, and she hugged it while riding the massive draft horse.

Eli finished discing in one direction and started over again from another angle. During the second pass, Matt asked, "Isn't that dangerous? Couldn't one of your little sisters fall off and get run over by that disc?"

"No." Eli seemed confident. "These horses have such broad backs; it wouldn't be that easy to slip off. And Dolly and Molly love my little sisters. They would stop instantly if they felt one of them falling."

He called to his sister, "Mary Anna, slide down like you're falling off." Eli kept his horses walking forward as Mary Anna carefully slid down off the huge horse. Molly froze in place. Dolly, noticing her teammate stop, also came to a standstill. Giggling, Mary Anna grabbed a generous handful of tall grass from near the fence and fed both horses a quick snack. Eli gently lifted his little sister back onto the old mare.

After they went over everything twice, Eli tied his horses to the fence. Mary Anna and Marcille stayed seated, way up on Dolly and Molly, jabbering to each other in Dutch. Eli asked, "Would you have a garden rake I could use?"

"Come down into my garage, I think there are a couple of rakes in there." Eli followed Matt inside and looked around as bright fluorescent lights flickered on. Matt noticed Eli looking at an old baseball glove. "That was mine. I used to play a lot when I was about your age." The older guy tossed it to the younger. "Try it on. Maybe you could buy a new one with the money you'll get from this landscaping job?" Eli tried on the mitt and looked at it with bright eyes. Matt had been wondering what an Amish boy would do with $400, and felt this was a chance to ask. "How do you plan to spend your money?"

Eli's eyes lit up and he looked excited as he explained. "I'm not old enough to have my own money. Our family will use it to pay bills." Matt studied the boy's face, trying to understand why a boy would be so cheerful about giving his hard-earned money to his family. Up until that moment, Matt had assumed Eli was working hard because he wanted the money. They headed back outside. Eli's sisters were jabbering with each other while sitting up on their massive horses. Matt told Eli, "I really like what your grandpa said about whispering to horses."

Eli smiled. "My grandpa used to say that little children notice every sound around them, they take in all the sights, and smells. As people get older they forget how to listen. People who yell all the time...." Eli stopped talking. He looked at Matt sideways, as if he worried that he might have said too much. Matt encouraged him, "Go on, this is really interesting."

"He said that some people only hear what is loud and forget how to listen. They stop seeing and feeling."

Mary Anna called to Matt, "We have a new baby calf!"

"Really?" Matt walked over beside Molly and looked up at the little girl. She was smiling and asked, "Do you want to come and see it?"

"Sure," Matt responded without thinking. As he followed the children over to their Amish farm, he worried that he would run into their dad. He felt that an Amishman would think it was silly for an adult to go to a neighbor's place to see a calf. However, as they headed over, he couldn't help but enjoy watching Eli drive his big horses, each with a little Amish girl on board.

They headed down through the beautiful apple orchard, past their garden. Eli's mom and third sister were hoeing between rows of growing green plants. Matt noticed they were barefoot. They both waved at him as he walked by. Eli unhooked his horses and drove them into the huge barn. He took Mary Anna off Molly and Marcille, the littlest sister, reached out her arms for Matt to help her off Dolly. The little girls were also barefoot. Their tiny feet pitter-pattered as they ran toward a stall deep inside the big barn. Matt followed, taking in rich aromas of cow, horse, hay and straw. He

25

glanced around nervously, expecting to see their dad lurking in the shadows. A large black and white cow stood in thick straw, with a miniature copy of herself lying at her feet. Eli swung open a heavy wooden gate and both little girls walked right in and began petting the calf. It stood up and let out a tiny, "Moo." The little girls giggled and looked at Matt to see what he thought of their new baby. He didn't know what to say. He finally came up with, "It's pretty fun to have a new baby around, huh?"

Eli smiled, "We'll have lots of fresh milk and cream now. Our cow had been dry for the past while." The little girls ran off chasing a few barn kittens and Eli shut the gate. He asked, "Do you want to help me take Molly and Dolly's harness off?"

"Sure." Matt watched what Eli did with Dolly's harness and tried to do the same with Molly's. He fumbled his way through it, and awkwardly carried the heavy pile to where Eli hung his half.

Eli handed Matt a curry comb and said, "You can brush Molly while I brush Dolly." The massive horses were tied to a manger full of hay, busily eating.

Matt cautiously approached the big mare and brushed her huge neck, back, belly, and hip. "How do I get to her other side?"

"Just walk around behind her. They won't kick."

Matt stepped behind Molly and looked at both horses' huge rumps. There wasn't enough room between Molly and Dolly for a man to stand. Their thick legs and giant hooves looked intimidating. Eli walked right behind Molly and tapped on her hip. He whispered, "Step over, girl." Molly sidestepped and Matt gathered his courage and walked in between the two enormous horses. He enjoyed brushing Molly's sleek black side, while breathing in a warm scent of horse. He found a certain thrill standing between two monstrous creatures. Nevertheless, a wave of relief swept over him as he stepped back out into the walkway.

"Thanks for showing me your new calf. I should head home now."

"Thank you for helping me brush my horses."

Matt walked out of the barn and up through the orchard. He could see all three little girls in the garden. It wasn't clear if they were playing or working. All at once Matt realized Eli's mom was only a short distance away, in the shadows of her apple orchard. It was dusk and he couldn't see her face. Matt wasn't sure if he should speak or act as though he didn't notice her. He couldn't think of what to say to an Amish woman, so he decided to walk on by. As he passed where she stood, he heard her speak quietly. "I know what you're doing."

Matt stopped walking and looked in her direction. He wasn't sure he had heard right, or what she meant, if he did understand her words. He assumed she was talking about how he was letting little Eli work so hard for a small amount of money. "I'm sorry?" He spoke his words as a question, as if to ask what she said, or meant.

"Eli is really enjoying doing your yard project. I guess I won't try to keep him from helping you."

"Thank you. He's a really good boy. You're raising him right. I will pay him when we're finished." Matt waited to see if she was going to say anything more, but she remained silent.

As he turned to walk away, he heard her say, very quietly, "He told me." A slight breeze floated through the orchard and sent blossom petals down like confetti. Eli's cow mooed and her calf answered. Matt walked across the field between Eli's home and his. It seemed to Matt as though he had traveled one hundred years back in time.

Chapter 5

CONVERSATIONS

I t rained all the next day. Matt was depressed at work, but not for the reason he expected. Instead of worrying about getting his house sold, he found he was mostly disappointed that he wouldn't get to see his buddy, Eli, and his beautiful horses. As he pulled into the garage, Matt saw some movement out of the corner of his eye. On further investigation, he found Eli turning over soil with a shovel near the house. "What are you doing?" Matt called out through the rain.

"I couldn't get close enough with my horses. We don't want this part near the house to look unfinished." Matt didn't say anymore; he hurried inside and changed clothes. He looked for a shovel and hustled out into the rain to help his little friend. Matt watched Eli's pattern. He pointed his shovel, jumped on it to drive it in, and then turned the soil all in one direction. He imitated the boy. When they finally turned over all of the edges, they stood under the back porch roof to get out of the rain. They didn't speak to each other right away, but watched the rain run off tree limbs and the old fence. After a bit, Eli cleared his throat and asked quietly. "Was she sick, or was it an accident?" The little Amish boy's face was wet and his eyes were dark and sad.

Matt wasn't sure who Eli was asking about. He tried to think it through but finally decided to ask, "Who do you mean?"

"Your wife."

There wasn't any way Matt could have been prepared for Eli's question. Even if he had known the boy would ask something like that a week ahead. "No, Eli, I've never had a wife."

Eli looked at Matt as if he didn't believe him, and then changed the subject. "We may have to wait a few days before we can harrow and sow grass seed."

Matt looked at little Eli, "I'm sorry you don't have your grandpa anymore." Eli's dark eyes looked sad, and he nodded, acknowledging Matt's words.

"Was he sick, or was it an accident?"

Eli shot a glance up at Matt. "My grandpa didn't die. We just can't see each other nowadays because my family left the Amish."

This time Matt wasn't sure if he believed Eli. He asked, "You don't go to the Amish church?"

"We go to the same church you go to. I said something to you last Sunday but you didn't hear me."

Matt questioned the boy, "Why do you still dress Amish and everything?"

"It takes some time to make that change. I wear my new clothes to church. If you see us there, you'll believe me."

Matt laughed awkwardly. "You might have to yell at me—I don't hear much unless it's loud."

Learning to Listen

Several days passed. Matt watched his yard slowly dry out with a few windy afternoons, some sunshine, and heat. He hoped Eli would drive his big black horses through the gate on Saturday, but it didn't come to pass.

Sunday morning Matt met up with his church buddy, Ernie. They sat together through morning services as usual. When the meeting was over, Matt and Ernie stood in the foyer and visited casually with acquaintances. While he was heading for the door, Matt heard a whisper. He turned and looked. A boy with dark eyes smiled and said, "You heard me!"

"Eli?" Matt studied the boy's face. His eyes were the same; however, everything else was so different. It seemed strange to see Eli without a straw hat and suspenders. Three little girls stood with him, all smiling at Matt as though they knew him well. Matt crouched down and said their names one by one. "Miriam, Mary Anna, and Marcille. Hello ladies." It didn't seem right to see the girls wearing modern clothes either.

Eli said, "This is my mom, Sony."

"Sunny?" Matt asked as he stood back up.

"Nope, Sony." Eli looked up at his mother.

"Hello, Sony." Matt shook her hand. He hesitated—her eyes looked so familiar. They were dark, almost black, and shiny. He saw sadness and wisdom in them, and concluded that her eyes were so similar to Eli's, that he recognized them. He quickly took back his hand, when he realized he had stopped shaking hers while thinking about her eyes.

She smiled and spoke. "My name is actually Grandpa Enos's name in reverse, s-o-n-e. Everyone has always called me, Sony."

Matt nodded an acknowledgement. "Eli is a fine young man, and he's doing a great job with my yard. In fact, I'm gonna be disappointed when our project is done." He looked at Eli. "I will have to hire you to help me with some other work around my place." Eli's dark eyes shined, and Sony's were sparkling, too. A man was standing a little way behind Sony. He didn't step forward but watched Matt talking to the little girls. Matt wondered if it was Eli's dad. He wanted to go have words with him, about letting Eli work like a man and then taking the money. Instead, he told the little girls, "I will see you, ladies, and Molly and Dolly tomorrow." They were all smiles.

Ernie drove to their usual restaurant for Sunday lunch. Matt rode along in silence. "What's eating you, bud?" Ernie asked.

"Did you see that family I talked to after church?"

"Yeah, who was that?"

"That was my Amish neighbors. Well, they used to be Amish. That boy is the kid I hired to do my landscaping project."

Ernie laughed. "The one who thought you meant $400 instead of $4000?" Matt nodded. Ernie asked, "Are you going to just give him $400 then?"

Matt didn't respond immediately, but thought for a moment. He recalled Eli's and his mother's dark friendly eyes. And then he remembered the man he saw standing behind Eli's mom at church, how he didn't even have the decency to introduce himself. Matt found an anger growing inside. He wanted to tell the guy off for letting Eli work so hard and then keeping all the money. It even angered Matt that Eli's dad left the Amish and took the boy away from his grandpa. Matt gave Ernie his answer. "Yeah, if they agreed to $400, that will be enough."

"That kid has a pretty good-looking mama, huh?"

"Yeah, she sure looked different in modern clothes."

Barefoot

On Sunday evening, a lonely feeling that had never entered Matt's heart crept into a secret part of his being. He tried to deny it to himself. He even reasoned, *I must be coming down with something. I just don't feel quite right.* He tried listening to music but nothing seemed interesting. He turned on his television but nothing satisfied his melancholy feeling. He stepped outside without wearing shoes late that evening. He told himself, "If I'm barefoot I can feel if my yard is getting dry enough for Eli to come back." His feet sank into soft dirt. He hadn't had that feeling since he was a boy. He walked a lap around his entire property line. He stopped at the old apple tree and listened for the sounds of Amish young folks singing hymns. He heard it faintly. It was so soft and far away that he doubted whether he was actually hearing it or imagining the sounds. He stood under his tree and looked toward Eli's home. He found himself imagining Eli's dad sitting in a bent-hickory rocking chair, reading something, while his wife cut pieces of homemade pie. Eli and his little sisters were probably playing an Amish card game or lying on their bellies on a hardwood floor, coloring quietly with crayons. As he watched a lantern flicker in his neighbor's kitchen window, Matt heard a calf bawl and clicking sounds come from a farther-away Amish farm. He concluded that it was the sound of pigs eating from feeders that had lids. He remembered watching hogs nose up feeder lids with their snouts, and when they backed away for a moment, a lid would slap back down. A horse trotted along the paved road in front of Matt's house. He listened as horseshoes made a nice clip-clopping sound, and buggy-wheels followed with a warm rumble.

Chapter 6

GOOD SEED

E li drove his horses around the edge of his cornfield. Matt walked out to see what he was doing and realized that tiny corn plants were emerging everywhere. Marcille, Eli's youngest sister, was riding on the flat implement that Molly and Dolly pulled on the field's edge. Sunshine beamed down brightly as the horses came through the old gate. "Where are your older sisters?" Matt asked Marcille.

Eli spoke a few words to her in Dutch and she replied to him in kind. Eli translated, "She says that Miriam and Mary Anna are helping our mom bake bread. But Eli needed me to help at Matt's."

"Does she understand English?" Matt asked in a whisper.

Eli nodded, "She understands a lot. She usually speaks Dutch but is learning English fast."

Little Marcille smiled and said, "Yes, fast!"

Eli added, under his breath, "Mom asked if I had a job for her." Then he spoke loud enough for Marcille to hear. "She is going to be a weight on my harrow, to help smooth your yard better." Marcille smiled really big and hugged her little doll, rocking it as she sat on a concrete block.

Matt laughed and told Eli, "She makes a good weight, probably adds another 25 pounds."

Eli whispered softly to his horses and they set off to work, toting Eli, Marcille, and a few concrete blocks on their harrow. Molly and Dolly made sweeping passes over every corner of Matt's yard. Rain had made a thin crust on the surface; however, Eli's harrow broke through and left a soft smooth finish. Matt used a hand rake to smooth out any edges that Eli couldn't reach with his implement. In a short time, everything was smooth. "Marcille and I will go get our seeder-wagon and come back to sow grass seed."

Matt's mom pulled in the drive while Eli was sowing grass seed. Miriam, Mary Anna, and little Marcille rode in the wagon box, making sure grass seed continually fed down in a steady stream.

Eli told Matt, "You have plenty of seed, so I feel like we should go over everything once, harrow, and then sow grass seed again."

While Eli and his sisters went back and forth, Matt's mom teased, "You are so good with children, Matt. I wish you would settle down, get married, and have a family."

"I don't want to have to try to make a wife happy. And I don't want the pressure of trying to provide for a family."

His mom frowned. "You have a good job; you could provide well enough. I can see how much those Amish kids like you. Wouldn't it be fun to be a dad?"

"It'd be great to have kids like these, but I couldn't raise children this good."

His mother shook her head in disappointment, got in her car, and left.

When the grass seed was all on the ground, Eli suggested that he and Matt gently rake the edges that his horses and harrow couldn't reach. "We have some old straw up in our hay mow. We should go get a few bales and cover everything up."

Matt rode along in the wagon with Eli and his sisters. It was a beautiful evening, perfect for riding in a wagon behind a team of horses. They rode down the hill through apple trees and backed into a large doorway of the big barn. Matt looked around for any sign of Eli's dad. He began to wonder if the guy was hiding from him or if he was sick or something. Eli tossed straw bales down onto the ground and Matt set them in the wagon. The little girls climbed up and sat on them. As they passed the house, Sony came out and waved at Matt.

Eli drove his horses over the yard while Matt and the girls dropped sections of straw on the ground. When they had spread it around, they all climbed out and shook the chunks and scattered straw evenly all over the yard. Matt and Mary Anna were a little distance from the others. She whispered, "Eli told us that we are going to make Matt's yard so nice he won't want to move away."

"I think he did that already," Matt whispered back.

Matt was disappointed when everything was finished. He didn't want his little friends to leave, not knowing when he would see them again. Eli pulled up with his beautiful black horses and said to his sisters, "We're done now, we should go home and not crowd out our neighbor."

"Oh, you're not crowding me out! Please feel free to come visit me anytime you want." He reached into his pocket and pulled out his checkbook.

Eli saw him and muttered, "I don't want to take your money. You're my friend."

"Ernie is my friend and he was going to take a lot more money from me for this same job. It's good for friends to hire their friends rather than someone else." Eli shrugged. Matt took out a pen and wrote Eli's name on the check. He didn't want to make it easy for his dad to cash it. He started to write $400, but glancing up at Eli and his sisters, he thought about all the work they had put into his project. He decided that he couldn't cheat them, even if Eli's dad took the money. He added a zero and folded the check, gave it to Eli, and shook his hand. "You did a great job, better than my buddy Ernie would've done! I guess I will see you all at church, if not out here in the field." They smiled and Eli whispered to his horses. Molly and Dolly headed slowly for the gate.

"Just a minute, Eli, I almost forgot something." Matt ran down into his garage and came back with his old baseball glove. He tossed it to Eli. "I want you to have that."

"I couldn't take it. Wasn't it yours when you were my age? You should give it to your own son someday." Eli reached it out to give back. Matt pushed it toward the boy. "Now, don't argue with me. I thought about it and I want you to have it." Matt knew that Eli was too well-mannered to talk back to an adult. His dark eyes lit up as he put it on and looked it over.

"Thanks for doing a great job with my yard. In fact, you did such nice work; I don't think I want to sell my house after all." Eli's eyes shined as he whispered to his horses. They leaned forward, through the gate, and back across the field.

Chapter 7

MEMORIES

Matt stood near the fence under his solitary apple tree—all that remained of his grandfather's farm. He thought about how he had planned to cut down his apple tree, until Eli talked him out of it. He looked at the old fence and it brought back memories of his grandpa's farm. Under the limbs of his old tree and leaning on that fence, something happened. In the twinkling of an eye, it came back to him. He had stood in that exact place as a boy, when he was about Eli's age. A gentle breeze blew across Eli's field and brought a scent of cattle and horses, dirt, and growing corn. Matt was transported through time by those sights and smells, and even the sound of a nighthawk that flew over his tree. He remembered that one night, as a boy, he stood in that same place, waiting for a girl to come and talk to him. He looked over at Eli's house. The skyline of that farm hadn't changed through all of those years. Everything seemed the same as that night, even the way the moon had a few faint clouds moving over its face.

"Sunny," that is what he remembered calling the little neighbor girl. The very girl that came out to meet him that night so long ago. In a flash he knew that the girl was Eli's mother, Sony. He stood staring at a lantern glowing from her kitchen window, wondering if she remembered him. Suddenly, he realized someone was walking across the field toward the gate. He strained his eyes to make out if it was a real person, or his imagination. First, he saw a white prayer cap with long strings dangling. Next, he could make out an Amish dress with a lighter colored apron. She walked slowly toward the gate as though she meant to go through it. Matt's mind raced. He didn't want her to see that he was standing under his apple tree, staring at her house. He tried to walk out nonchalantly and spoke, "Sony?"

Right at the opening of the gate she stopped like a statue. He said it again. "Sony, it's me, Matt. I was just looking over my yard and what a good job Eli did." She walked down the fence row, on her side of the divide. Deja' vu was running rampant. He clearly remembered calling out her name years ago as she walked out to meet him.

"Hello, Matt." She held out her hand. He could barely see by moonlight that she was holding out a small paper. "I can't take it," she said.

"What, the check?" Matt asked.

"Yes—it's too much." She held the check at arm's length, even though he didn't move to get it.

Matt told her, "Eli might have thought I said $400, but I meant $4000. My friend Ernie has a landscaping business and he was going to charge me more than that." He watched to see if she would keep it. She lifted her apron to her face. He couldn't tell for sure, but it seemed she was covering her face and crying. Matt didn't know what to say to a woman in tears. He just stood leaning on the fence, under his apple tree, feeling awkward. Her shoulders slumped, and then he saw her sit on the ground and rest her forehead on her knees. She covered her head with her arms and hands and sobbed for a while. Matt scolded himself, inside, for not knowing what to say or do.

At last he spoke in a whisper, "Are you okay?"

Sony took out a hanky and blew her nose into it. She cleared her throat and asked in a pathetic, small voice. "Did our church put you up to this?"

"No."

"I have to tell you ever since my husband's death, I have been wondering if we made a mistake to leave the Amish. I didn't go back because I thought everyone will say that Joe did wrong. Inside I doubted people at our new church if they even cared, or would help. They didn't give us anything. I knew that if we were still Amish they would have taken good care of us."

Matt listened quietly but he was struggling to understand what she was saying, and trying to take in the part about her husband's death. She continued to talk, but he stopped her.

"Just a minute, Sony—are you saying that Eli's dad died?"

"Yes, about a year ago. Ever since Joe's death, Eli has tried so hard to make me happy. He works hard to provide for his family, even though I tell him that he needs to play like other boys his age. He hasn't had any male role model in his life since that time. Until ... you came along." Matt was speechless. Sony continued, "I can't begin to say what a change I've seen in Eli since he became your friend. He was sad for a whole year; now, I see him smile again."

Matt's eyes stung, and then hot tears began to stream down his own cheeks. He couldn't speak. Sony added quietly, from her seat on the ground, "After what you have done, I know that there are good people among the English."

Matt wiped his eyes on his sleeve. "Sony, I've got some bad news for you. I'm not as good of a person as you think I am. I didn't want to tell you this, but...." He hesitated to think of a good way to explain the truth. "The first time I saw Eli, I yelled at him for hauling manure too close to the fence."

"I've told him not to go close to the neighbors with that manure!" She seemed upset.

"Sony, what I'm trying to say is that Eli is the nicest young man I've ever met. I feel bad because I hollered at him, and I also planned to let him do all of that work for only $400, because I thought he was just a kid. Then, when you said to me, 'I know what you're doing,' I thought that you were accusing me of cheating him."

Sony laughed. "I was saying that I knew you were giving him a job just to help us."

"I wish I were that good of a man, but I'm not."

"You are a better man than you think. Once you got to know Eli, you cared about him and talked to him. That shows what kind of a man you are. I don't think that we will go back to the Amish. You've given us reason to believe that we can make it."

"This may be a funny thing to say, but because of your son Eli, I found myself wishing that I could become Amish." Matt stared at Sony in the darkness. She didn't speak but let out a cute giggle. He spilled out a question that had been on his mind. "I don't understand why your family still dresses Amish and lives that lifestyle if you already left the church?"

"My husband had his heart set on going to the church you go to." She was silent for a moment as if choking back tears, and then continued. "Only, a short time after we changed churches, he was killed in an accident. I didn't know what to do...." Her voice trailing off in a sweet, sad way that made Matt's eyes tear up again as she wept.

"Us English people just aren't raising our children as good as our Amish neighbors," Matt told her. Sony laughed and wiped her eyes again. Matt continued, "Eli misses his grandpa so much. That man has taught your son so many good things, and Eli has been teaching me what his grandpa taught him. I think you should consider going back to the Amish." Matt looked at Sony. He could barely see her as she sat in the grass near the fence. He worried that he had said too much. He tried to imagine what she was going through, being alone in the world, and raising a family. He wanted to say something encouraging. "Sony, you don't have to make a decision tonight about the future. In the meantime, I want you to keep my check; Eli earned every penny of it. I also want you to know that I am here to help you and your family any way I can. I think that you are doing an outstanding job of raising your children. I've never met such nice children in all of my life."

Sony stood up and wiped her hands on her apron. She reached across the fence and shook Matt's hand. "Thank you for everything."

"Do you remember meeting me under this tree when we were about Eli's age?" he asked.

"Yes," she whispered, and headed across the field. Matt watched her disappear into the milky twilight. Under the glowing moon, he remembered that as a boy, he had played with grandpa's neighbor children. He didn't know that they were Amish; he just thought of them as farm kids. They chased rabbits, climbed trees, and tried to build a beaver dam down in the creek. He and a girl that was about his age always stayed near each other. As he reminisced about those days, he could still see her dark, shiny eyes and quick smile. He remembered wanting to talk to her when her brothers weren't around and telling her, "Meet me by this apple tree, at dusk."

"Okay," was all she said, and he didn't know if she would show up. While he had waited for her, he carved the words, "Sunny + Matt" on the tree trunk.

Matt stopped his memories long enough to run his hand along the tree's coarse bark, feeling for words. Sure enough he could feel them, still there after all of those years. It came flooding back to him, how he had shown her what he had carved. In the dimness of that night, so long ago, their names were barely visible, as was her smile. He recalled it being just dark enough that night to give him the courage to say, "Someday, I'm going to marry you." He smiled as he remembered her whispering, "Okay."

Other books written by Thomas Nye:
Under the Heavens, Amish Horses Series Book I
Catbird Singing, Amish Horses Series Book II

Thomas Nye is the author of the Amish Horses Book Series. His writing focuses on two of his main interests, Amish and draft horses. In the Amish Horses Book Series, a teenage city boy spends summers with his Amish relatives. He has many extraordinary adventures and even finds a little romance, working in the fields of his uncle's farms.

For more information visit:
Thomas Nye's blog: amishhorses.blogspot.com
Or write: Amish Horses P.O. Box 495 Kalona, Iowa 52247